KU-661-096

FLUFF
and other stuff

ORCHARD BOOKS
96 Leonard Street, London EC2A 4XD
Orchard Books Australia
Unit 31/56 O'Riordan Street, Alexandria, NSW 2015
First published in Great Britain in 2001
ISBN 1 84121 813 8

A CIP catalogue record for this book
is available from the British Library
10 9 8 7 6 5 4 3 2 1
Printed in Great Britain

FLUFF and other stuff

poems by TONY MITTON

pictures by PHILIP HOPMAN

ORCHARD BOOKS

To Megan Larkin
and children with pockets, everywhere
TM

To Maggie
PH

Contents

Poem In My Pocket

In my pocket,
feeling round,
what can this be
that I've found?

Pull it out to see
and...oooh!
Look: a poem
just for you.

String

I'm knotty.
I'm grotty.
I'm in a
twisty
    tangle.
A piece
of string,
I'm just
the thing
to make
a conker
    dangle.

Twang!

I love to stretch
and pluck you – twang!

I pull you back
to flick – f'tang!

Rubber ribbon,
stretchy strand,
you are my own
e______ b___.

Answer: elastic band

Tissue

Scrumpled up and worn,
a bit tattered and torn,

it's time to put you in the bin –
hmmm…can't see one to put you in.

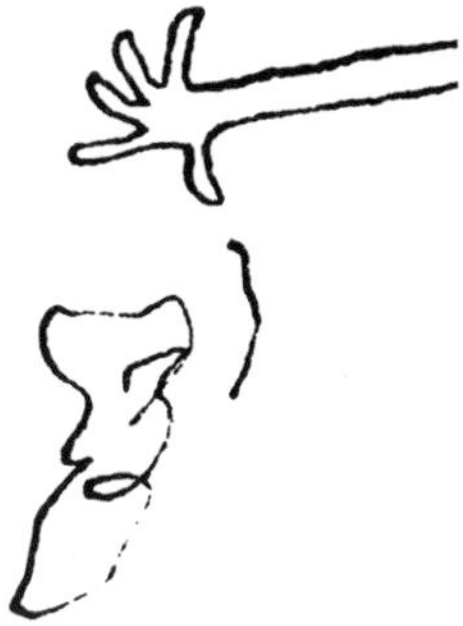

A quick wipe of the nose –
here goes…

then back you go, scruff,
with bits and bobs and strands of fluff,

screwed up with all the other stuff.

Sweet

Although you are smooth and creamy,
although you are sugary sweet,
although you are wrapped like a present,
although you're delicious to eat,

you're down in the dark of my pocket
as if you're a nugget of treasure.
I'm saving you up for a magical moment,
so as to double the pleasure.

I'm keeping you safe in my pocket,
as I do with the things that I get.
I'm saving you up for a special occasion.
I'm not going to eat you…yet!

Silver Foil

Crinkly, crunkly,
shimmery, shiny,
scrap of foil
so small and tiny,

used to wrap
a chocolate bar,
but in my pocket
you've come far.

I roll you in
a ball, and soon
you turn into
my silver moon.

Cracker ring

The cracker burst open –
flash! crack!

Something flew out
as I tumbled back.

There by my foot
was a glittery thing.

Could it be? Yes…
a little gold ring.

Well, actually plastic,
and coloured golden,

and probably not very
precious or olden.

But perhaps if I wear it
in secret, at night,

a genie will visit.
I think it might.

Germ

Ghost bug,
invisible,
it makes me wince and squirm
to think that in my pocket squats
a germ.

Flea

Tee hee!
It's me.
A tiny flea.
The itchy patch
you have to scratch.

Tee hee!
It's me.
A tiny flea.
Just see me jump now.
Ready…?
Wheeeeeeeeeeee!

Swap Card

Down in my pocket...
what's this here?
It's one of those cards
from back last year.

Don't you remember?
Wow! What a craze!
It seems we've all
forgotten that phase.

Nobody wants these
any more.
I can't think what
I keep this for?

Key

This is the key.
The mystery key.

The key to what?
I'm not
quite sure.
I wonder what
this key is for?

Let me see…
could it be:

The key to the door
of a treasure store?

The key to a lid
where things lie hid?

A secret box
with magic locks?

The key to a cupboard,
a closet, a drawer?

I wonder what
this key is for?

When I find it
I'll unlock it,

but meanwhile keep
this key
in my pocket.

Pencil Sharpener

Down in the depths of my pocket
sits a sharpener shaped like a rocket.
It should sharpen each lead
but it snaps them instead
so the points all get stuck and just block it.

Pencil Stub

Just how long will a pencil last?
When is a pencil's lifetime past?
This one's down to an inch and a half.
I know it's small, but please don't laugh.
So long as its lead can still draw a line,
this old pencil's doing just fine.
Besides, it's sucky – and it's mine.

Rubber

Grubby little rubber,
grimy and grey,
with all of your corners
worn right away…

Grubby little rubber
growls, "Mind what you say.
I may be grimy
and worn and grey,

but I'm still quite strong.
I'm stubby, but I'm stout.
So watch your words
or I'll rub them out."

Bottle-top

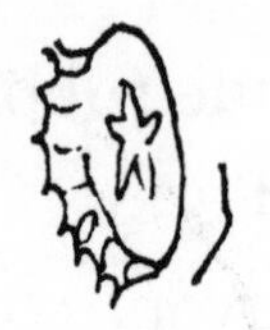

Psshht! went the top
of Dad's bubbly beer.

You clinked on the table
and then you were here:

a bottle-top
just like a coin
from a stash
of jewels and goblets
and treasure-chest cash.

I'll make a collection,
yes, that'll be fun.

Soon I'll have hundreds.
But you're Number One.

Button

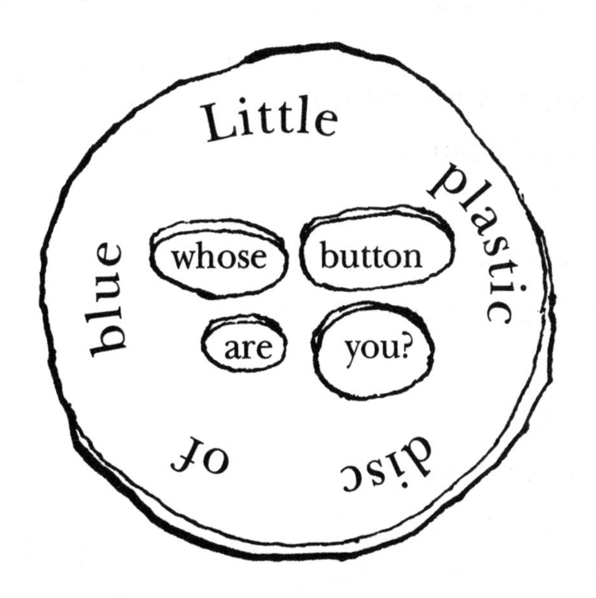

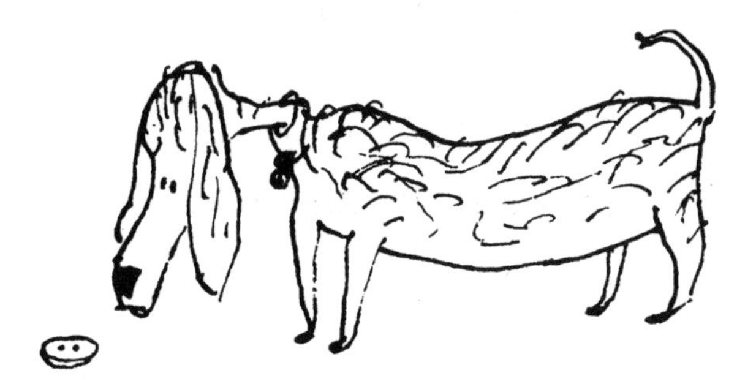

Name-tag

My name in dark blue
on a small white cotton tag
sits in my pocket.
I have my name-tag, oh yes,
but where has my sweatshirt gone?

Badge

I am the badge
that proves your swimming strength.

I am the badge
that states you swam one length.

I am the badge
that says you didn't sink

or stop off half-way there
to take a drink.

Paper-clip

I may be tiny
but I've got grip.

Set me to work
and I rarely slip.

Pages I clamp
with my silver lip.

I am a shiny
paper-clip.

Mystery Object

I don't know where you came from.
I don't know what you are.
Maybe you came from a camera,
or a radio, or a car?

I don't know what your name is.
I don't know what you do.
In all my life I've never seen
a thing shaped quite like you.

So I'll keep you in my pocket
as a puzzling mystery bit.
And, who knows? Maybe one day
I'll find out where you fit.

Screw

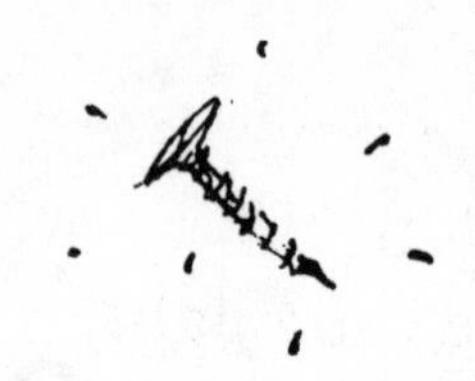

Very important
tiny screw,

I know there's something
that you ought to do.

Somewhere
there's a hole
where you belong.

You ought to be there
keeping something strong.

Until I find
the thing you ought to do,
screw,
I'm holding on to you.

Until I find
the place you ought to be,
I'll keep you in my pocket,
close to me.

Ticket

Small piece of paper,
you are the memory of
a bus ride I took.

Dice

Roll a dice, bowl a dice
over the table.

Click a dice, flick a dice,
quick as you're able.

Swirl a dice, whirl a dice,
twirled like a top.

See if you've won
when it's spun to a stop.

A quick dice flicker
flicks quicker than a snicker.

A quicker dice flicker
flicks fast as a fly.

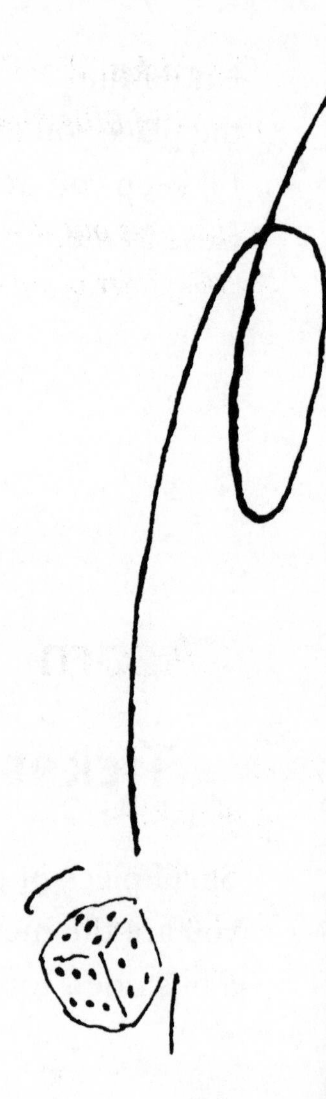

The quickest dice flicker
is a tricky little flicker,

as he flicks out a six
in the flicker of an eye!

Acorn

A
Carriable
Oak tree
Rolled up in a
Nut

Marble

Blue glass marble,
rough and round,
made for rolling
on the ground,

chipped and pitted,
cracked and old,
often pitched
and tossed and rolled,

your glassy sphere
of midnight blue
held up to light
reveals to view

a dreamy cave
so deep and wide
it seems that I
could drift inside.

I hold you to
my open eye,
and when I view
your blue, I sigh…

Magnifying Glass

Little piece
of magic glass,
for watching insects
as they pass,
stumbling through
the jungly grass.

Through your window
bug, leaf, twig,
seem to grow
so very big.

You came free
in a cornflake packet.
Now I keep you
in my pocket.

Feather

a bird-dresser
a wind-presser

a pillow-filler
a poet-quiller

an arrow-aimer
a dust-tamer

a cobweb-breaker
a tickle-maker

a headdress-sticker
a pocket-pricker

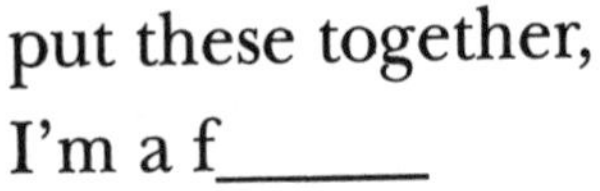

put these together,
I'm a f______

Answer: feather

Coin

It may not be silver, or gold,
but this coin
is a coin that I like to hold.
For here, on the front,
is a tropical tree,
the kind that you get
by a calm, warm sea.
And it seems to me,
that long, long ago
and far, far away
was a place where this coin
could be used to pay
for fruit or for honey
or for bright, fresh fish.

So sometimes I hold it
and dream and wish
I could be on the beach
by that tropical tree,
with long ago, far away
things to see.

Shell

Curly, coily
shell,
will you whisper,
will you tell
the spell
that's wound around
or spiralled secretly
inside you?

Tiny, shiny
shell,
I found you
on the beach
and put you
in my pocket
in the hope
that you might teach
to me

strange secrets
of the sea.

Silent shell,
if I listen
will you tell?
Well...?

Pebble

Little pebble, tiny stone,
you were lying all alone

till I kicked you with my shoe.
That was when I noticed you.

I picked you up, blew off the dust.
I felt I had to, felt I must.

Little pebble, tiny stone,
now you are my special one.

I like to tuck you in my fist.
If I lost you, you'd be missed.

Tamagoochi

Coochy, coochy
Tamagoochi.

Be my baby
sweet and choochy.

In my pocket
you can sleep.

When you wake
I'll hear you bleep.

Then I'll change
your cyber-nappy,

press your buttons,
make you happy.

You're my choochy
cyber-chappy.

Hole

Now that my fingers
have found you,
I know
that you will grow.

Little o
                -pening,
rubbed by bits and bobs,
fiddled by fingers,

you will grow like so...
until oh,
bless my soul!

What a big hole!

Tea Card

On this card
from a packet of tea
there's a very strange creature
from under the sea.
It looks just like
a monster to me.
It's ever so ugly
and scary to see.
It's slippy and slimy
and covered in goo.
And it's here in my pocket
just to show...YOU!

List

Here is a list
of things I hope to get…
although I guess
there's not much chance,
just yet:

a tiny, intelligent
talking mouse,

a CD player
that shakes the house,

a pair of trainers
worth a grand,

the best computer
in all the land,

a luxury limousine,
sleek and long,

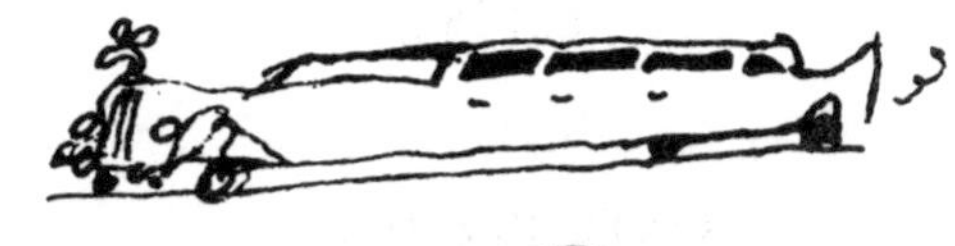

a boa constrictor,
really strong,

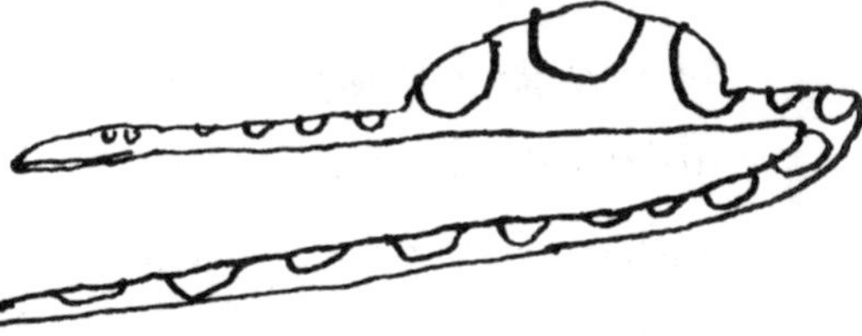

a swanky holiday
somewhere hot,

a hoard of chocolate,
yes, a lot!

a baby dragon
in a fire-proof hutch,

and a mini-mobile
to stay in touch,

oh, and here at the end,
just in case,
for other things
a nice
big
space:

Fluff

What's this here?
A piece of fluff.

I don't know where
I get this stuff.

I'll blow it away
with just one puff.

Huff!

There. That's enough.

Pick up a Poem
with another Orchard poetry book!

Zoo of Dreams
poems by Adrian Mitchell
pictures by Peter Bailey
ISBN 1 84121 817 0

Come Back to me my Boomerang
poems by John Agard
pictures by Lydia Monks
ISBN 1 84121 748 4

The Box Room
poems by Sophie Hannah
pictures by Helen Stephens
ISBN 1 84121 793 X